Claire: A Mormon Girl
Book I: Claire in Zarahemla

by Paris Anderson

cover and illustrations
by Velva Campbell

A Precious Child Publication
1356 East Oak Crest Lane
Provo, Utah 84604

ISBN 1-56684-051-1

Acknowledgements:

The author would like to thank the following people for the inspiration, encouragement and assistance they have so generously offered: Patricia Anderson, Dixon Anderson, Helen Anderson, Jack Anderson, Robert Canaan, Scott Roberts, Lindon Parks, Robert Spanvill, Larry Rowland and Lana Rowland.

Table of Contents:

Claire: A Mormon Girl

Book I: Claire in Zarahemla

Prologue

THIS is a story about Claire Nicol. She is a twelve-year-old girl who was born in Lanark County in Upper Canada (now called Ontario). Her mother was also born in Canada, the daughter of a wealthy cattleman and granddaughter of a French fur trapper. Her father was born in Scotland and joined the British Army at the age of fifteen. He was sent to Canada and served for ten years in Quebec before he was released from the service. After leaving the army, he traveled to Upper Canada and found a job at *The Lanark Star*, a newspaper there. He married and soon twin daughters, named Claire and Marie, were born.

The young family lived very happily until Claire and Marie were six-years-old. Then one terrible winter both girls got scarlet fever. They were in bed for months, and every doctor in the whole county said there was no hope for them; they would soon die. But Mr. Nicol was a religious man, and he prayed day and night that his two little girls might be spared.

The Lord heard these fervent and sincere prayers and restored the girls to health. But, as often happens with scarlet fever, Marie didn't recover fully and was left with a weak heart.

When the girls were eight-years-old, they spent the day at their Grandfather Molineaux's stockyards to help take care of the orphaned calves. The girls overexerted themselves, and Marie, with her weakened heart, got sick again and passed away.

Gloom and despair fell upon the family like the blackest of all shadows. Claire felt like half of her soul had been taken away from her.

Not even the birth of Jacques, a new baby brother, could erase their depression.

But one day, when Claire was eleven-years-old, Mr. Nicol was setting type for the newspaper, and he noticed a report in the paper that announced a series of sermons to be given by missionaries of a new religion called The Church of Jesus Christ of Latter-Day Saints. When he went home for dinner that evening, Mr. Nicol told Claire and her mother about the report. His eyes were very bright as he spoke, and for the first time since Marie had passed away, his heart was joyful. Claire got very excited about going to hear the sermons, but her mother wanted nothing to do with any "new" religion.

So Claire and her father went to hear the sermons alone, and when they returned home that evening, they were even more excited than when they had left. Mr. Nicol was at the point of tears as he tried to explain to his wife what the missionaries of this new religion had taught. He sat down in a chair and started to cry even before he came to the best part.

"My heart is burning with glory and joy!" he said, holding his fist to his chest. "I know this religion is right for us!"

"And the best part," Claire said, putting one hand on her father's shoulder, "was when the missionaries talked about families. They said when their new temple gets built, families can go there and get sealed. And that means when we go to Heaven, Marie will be waiting for us!"

Mrs. Nicol's mouth dropped open and her lips began to quiver. A tear fell from one eye. Without a word she ran to the bedroom and wrapped Jacques in a blanket.

"Let's go find those missionaries," she said when she came back to the parlor. "I want to hear their sermon."

Though it was almost midnight, the family ran to the house where the missionaries were staying and woke them up. Mrs. Nicol insisted that they give the whole sermon again, so she could hear it from start to finish.

Mrs. Nicol was very impressed with the sermon the missionaries gave that night, and together the family attended all of the other sermons. They were baptized a month later.

Grampa Molineaux, Mrs. Nicol's father, became so angry that his daughter would leave the old religion that his heart broke, and he never spoke to her or her family again, though he loved them dearly. This was very hard on Claire, because they had always been best friends and often told little secrets to each other. That winter Grampa Molineaux got pneumonia and died. Claire cried for weeks because she never even got to say good-bye.

In the fall of 1842, just after Claire's twelfth birthday, Mama found out she was going to have another baby, and Papa decided that it was time for the family to gather with the Saints in a city called Nauvoo, Illinois, which stood on the eastern bank of the Mississippi River. That winter Papa sold everything they had, and in the early spring they set out.

The family traveled to the Great Lakes by way of coach, then crossed the lakes to Chicago on a steamship. They traveled in another coach a hundred miles to Dixon and hired a skiff to carry them down the Little Rock River to the Mississippi. There Papa secured passage on a stern-wheel riverboat all the way to Nauvoo.

It was expensive to travel on coaches, steamships, skiffs and riverboats, but Papa was eager to spend his hard-earned money. He was afraid that Claire, like Marie, had a weak heart and would get sick and die if she overexerted herself again. Besides, Mama was in no condition to walk from Upper Canada to Nauvoo, either.

When the family arrived in Nauvoo they were almost destitute. With the little money they had left, Papa bought a small piece of land in Nauvoo and rented a tiny cabin in a village called Zarahemla a mile from the western bank of the Mississippi.

This book, which is the first in a series of five, takes place in the summer of 1843 and is the story of the birth of Claire's newest baby brother.

Other important characters in this story are:

William Smith--younger brother of the Prophet Joseph Smith and editor-in-chief at *The Wasp*, a newspaper in Nauvoo.

Sister Jones--the only midwife who lives in Zarahemla.

Brother Jones--Sister Jones' husband.

Sister O'Brien--a midwife who lives in Nauvoo.

Brother O'Brien--a ferryman. He is Sister O'Brien's husband.

Brother Green--owner of the fastest team of horses in Nauvoo.

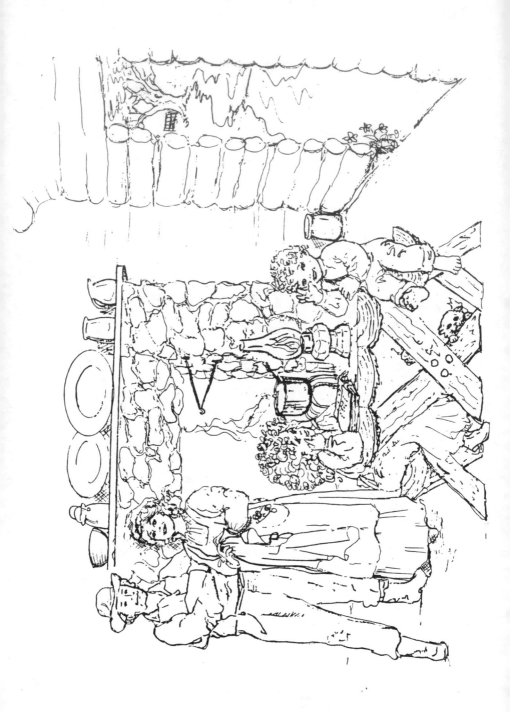

Chapter One

IT was still early when twelve-year-old Claire went with her father to the river, but already the early July sun drenched her. Her calico dress made the heat worse. Papa didn't seem to notice the heat. His tattered linen shirt already had dark patches of sweat on the neck and back, but Papa acted as if he didn't mind.

Brother Nicol, Claire's father, worked at *The Wasp*, a weekly newspaper in Nauvoo, and had to cross the river at least three times a week. Every time he went over he brought Claire along on horseback as far as the river, saying the fresh air would do her good. And every time he got in his canoe to cross the river, he ordered Claire to go straight home and not get off the horse on the way.

Claire swatted the back of one hand. A small bug was pasted to her palm. She wiped it off on the horse's neck.

Mosquitos usually didn't come out into the blaring sunlight. They usually stayed under the trees where it was cool. When Brother Nicol walked through a thicket of trees and pulled the horse into the shade, the mosquitos were as thick as rain. Brother Nicol didn't seem to notice the insects, but Claire and the horse both went crazy. Claire constantly swatted her face, neck and wrists. And Jezebel, the horse, whipped her tail back and forth and made her skin shimmy.

Claire noticed tiny beads of sweat beginning to form on the old black mare's neck.

"Papa," she said hesitantly, "I think ol' Jezebel is getting tired. Maybe I should get off and walk."

"Now Claire," Brother Nicol said, "you know how your mother and I feel about things like that."

"Yes, Papa."

Claire hung her head slightly and bit her tongue.

"Beautiful day, isn't it, Claire?" Brother Nicol said after a moment.

"Yes, Papa."

"I think I'll write an editorial about the beauties of the natural world for *The Wasp*. Creating such a beautiful place where we can live and learn was probably one of God's greatest gifts, don't you think?"

"Yes, Papa."

"I'll have to talk to Brother William Smith about such an editorial first. I'll have to get permission."

Brother Nicol led the black mare through a grove of trees to a shallow cove in the river bank. Claire started swatting furiously, and Jezebel's skin shimmied like the wind in a wheat field. There was a small canoe and several logs floating in the cove.

Brother Nicol had punctured the canoe on a submerged log several months ago, when he first started working for *The Wasp*. He had to carry the canoe all the way home, and two days went by before he could fix it.

"I'm going to have to clear those logs out some day," Brother Nicol said. He gave the reins to Claire.

"Papa, why do we come so far up the river when you cross over to Nauvoo?"

"Well, the current in the Mississippi is slow, but the river's so wide that my canoe will be carried a mile downstream before I get to the other side. So, if I walk a mile upstream before I launch, then the current will take me straight into Nauvoo. Think like a Scotsman, lass."

Brother Nicol pulled the rope on the canoe to draw it closer to shore and started to get in.

"Papa," Claire quickly asked, "may I go with you? I've never seen a printing press before."

"No, we're very busy printing pamphlets and posters for the Fourth of July celebration the day after tomorrow. You'd just be in the way."

"I wouldn't be, Papa--I promise! You're always saying you need a good proofreader at *The Wasp*, and you known I can read better than most grown-ups."

"Aye, that you can, but you've a feeble heart and you couldn't make it all the way there. After I cross the river, I've still got to walk another mile to get into town." Papa knelt in the back of the canoe.

"But, Papa," Claire said in a whiny tone, "I don't have a weak heart--I'm strong!"

"Your mother and I already lost one child and we're not going to lose another."

"But, Papa, I won't get sick again--I promise!"

"I said no, lass. Now you go home and don't get off that horse."

Claire bowed her head slightly and fell silent. Brother Nicol pushed off from the shore, then waved as the current carried the boat downstream.

Papa was always saying that--"we've already lost one child and we're not going to lose another."

Claire and her twin sister, Marie, both had scarlet fever when the family lived in Canada. They seemed to recover well, but one day Marie went on a long walk on Grampa Molineaux's farm. Marie got sick again and died a week later. Since that day Mama and

Papa had treated Claire like a two-day-old baby.

Don't do this, Claire, you might get sick. Don't do that. . ..

They did all the work around the house and made Claire sit in a chair by the window all day long and practice sewing. They didn't even let her go to the school at Sister Knight's house. Now that her mother was expecting a baby and the midwife told her to stay in bed all day, Brother Nicol did most of the work around the house besides his own work.

I'm not a baby, Claire thought angrily, *and come the Fourth of July I'll prove it!*

As soon as her father was out of sight Claire got off of the horse and started walking back the way they came.

"We'll show him, won't we, Jezebel?"

The horse snorted.

"I'll win all of the foot races at the Fourth of July celebration, and then he'll know I don't have a weak heart."

Claire reached between her ankles and grabbed the hem of the back of her skirt and pulled it up to her waist in front, making britches.

"Come on," she said to the horse, "let's race."

Claire had been running back from the cove for almost two months now. When she first started she could only run a few hundred yards before she had to stop and rest. But now she could run almost all the way home. The only time she had to stop was when Jezebel would

 fall too far behind and she would have to wait for the horse to catch up. Jezebel was a year older than Claire and she was

blind in one eye, so Claire had to stop and wait two or three times every mile.

Claire enjoyed running. The mosquitos never bothered her then; they couldn't catch her. The cool breeze on her creamy face was so delicious, and her long curly black hair bounced at every stride. Sometimes Claire imagined that she was part of the breeze herself, playing tag with flying birds and carrying puffs of milkweed into the river.

Claire glanced over her shoulder. Jezebel was nowhere in sight. She sat on a rock where the sun was bright and waited.

Nauvoo was in plain sight from where she sat. Most buildings there were first houses-- wooden shacks with uneven plank walls. A few of the buildings were glorious brick structures called big houses. That's where rich people or long-time residents lived. Papa bought land in Nauvoo when the family first arrived from Canada and started to build a big house. But when the midwife told Mama to stay in bed for the rest of her time waiting for the baby, he rented a small, old log cabin across the river in Zarahemla.

Jezebel trotted into sight.

"You see that grand building over there on the hill, Jezebel?" Claire yelled. "That's the Temple. It's not finished yet, but when they're done, Papa, Mama, me and little Jacques will go there and get sealed. Marie will be sealed to us, too, and that way we can be twins again. Last winter, before Mama was in the family way, they let us go into the basement, and I was baptized for her."

The old horse snorted its approval.

"Are you ready to race again?" Claire said, grabbing the hem of her dress again. She didn't stop running until she came to a small grove a few hundred yards from the cabin. She waited there for several minutes before the old mare appeared.

"Sometimes I think you let me win, Jezebel," Claire said, climbing onto the horse's back. "Either that or maybe you're stopping to eat the flowers."

They started toward the cabin.

Chapter Two

MAMA was kneeling in front of the fireplace when Claire opened the front door. She was piling hot ashes on a loaf of boiled corn meal on the hearth. Four-year-old Jacques was sitting in the corner quietly playing with a top Papa had carved for him.

"I'll do that, Mama," Claire quickly said. "You go lay down like the midwife ordered."

"Now, Claire," Sister Nicol said, "you know how your father and I feel about you working around the house all the time."

"Yes, Mama, I know," Claire said in an irritated tone. "You're afraid I'll get sick again, and you're afraid you'll lose me like you lost Marie."

"That's right."

"But, Mama, if you don't go to bed and eat a lot of meat like the midwife said, you might lose the baby. You might even have complications and die."

"I suppose that's true. That's what the midwife said."

"All right then. If you go back to bed and let me fix the ash-cake for Jacques, I'll finish sewing that shirt today. I won't even stop unless Jacques needs me."

"All right. . .if you promise."

"I promise."

Sister Nicol slowly stood, pulling herself up with a hand on the mantle of the fireplace. She walked slowly to her bedroom, stepping carefully to avoid tripping on the uneven warped planks.

Mama had been a slender, willowy woman before she got in the family way, but now she was, as Papa said, "pleasantly plump." In the last seven months she had gained almost thirty pounds, and none of her dresses fit anymore. All day long she wore her white linen night clothes. But Mama didn't need other clothes. She hadn't left the house once in the past four months and had rarely left her bed.

"Mama, you go to bed now?" Jacques asked.

"Yes, I'm going to bed now."

"I'm hungry, Mama!"

"Claire will fix your ash-cake. I have to rest."

Claire walked over to the fireplace and piled another scoop of hot ashes on loaf. Jacques walked over to her side to watch.

"Do you know what this is, Jacques?" she asked, pointing to a large cooking pot with a flat lid and three long legs.

"It's a spider!" Jacques answered in an excited tone.

"That's right, and do you know how it got it's name?"

"You told me one day ago, but I forgot."

"Then I'll tell you again. A long, long time ago there was an ordinary black garden spider named Hemish."

"That's a silly name!" Jacques said laughing.

"That's a name from Scotland, the country where Papa grew up. That's what he wants to name the baby, if it's a boy. Mama wants to name it "Pierre." That's a name from France. That's where Mama's parents were born.

"So anyway, Hemish was a curious spider. He was kind to all the other animals. When they would break a wing or a leg, he would always spin a web around the broken limb like a cast. One day a wicked witch came to the garden. She said, "Hemish, since you don't act like a true spider, I'm going to put a hex on you. From now on you'll never look like a true spider again. I'll make you go live with the cruel, cruel human-people. They'll throw you into the fire and pile hot coals on top of you. . .. So that's how this pot got its name."

"That's a silly story!" Jacques said.

"That's right, and you're a silly boy."

Jacques giggled.

"Now then, Jacques," Claire said, "you go outside and play with your top, and I'll call you when the ash-cake is ready."

Jacques went to get his top, then went out the front door. Claire uncovered a small portion of the ash-cake and touched it. It was only warm, but would soon be hot. She stood up and reached for two dishes sitting on the pegs imbedded in the wall--one for Mama and one for Jacques. Claire wasn't hungry. She had already eaten with Papa when he got up early this morning to go to

The Wasp. She took the jar of dark molasses off a shelf and set it on the table.

"Jacques has never had real sugar," Claire mumbled, "so he actually likes this."

She sat in the only chair and looked at the sewing basket disdainfully. The sight was too unkind to bear. She looked around the cabin to see if there was anything else she could do first. The uneven plank floor had already been swept. The oil-paper in the windows wasn't torn and didn't need to be replaced. The dishes were all arranged neatly on the pegs in the wall. There was nothing Claire could do other than sew. She put the sewing basket on the table and began threading a needle.

The shirt Claire was making was almost finished. It was for William Smith, the editor at *The Wasp.* After that, Sister Smith, his wife, wanted a nightgown sewn. Papa always asked rich people if they needed any sewing done. If they did, Mama would sew for them at a price.

But since the midwife sent her to bed, Claire did all of the sewing, even though she hated the work and her stitches were not as neat as Mama's.

Papa made barely enough money at *The Wasp* to pay the lease on the cabin, make payments on the land for the big house in Nauvoo and buy winter feed for Jezebel and the cow. Anything extra, like molasses for Jacques or meat for Mama, had to be paid for with money from sewing.

The front door slowly cracked open.

"Is it ready?" Jacques asked in a quiet voice.

Claire set the cloth and needle in the basket and set it on the floor.

"It's just ready now," she said, rising from the table. "Come and sit down."

Jacques threw the door open and rushed in.

"Careful not to trip!"

Jacques slowed to a fast walk. He sat in the chair and pulled a dish in front of himself.

Claire uncovered the ash-cake and dusted it off as best she could. With a clean damp rag she wiped off the remainder of the ashes. She cut a thick slice onto each plate, then poured molasses on each. She set a tall glass of water at the side of Jacques' dish.

Jacques started eating immediately, not waiting to give thanks. Claire smiled. She took a fork and the other plate to her mother's bedroom, the only other room in the house. She knocked softly, then entered. Mama was sleeping, so Claire just set the plate on the floor where she would see it and left.

Jacques had cleaned the ash-cake off his plate and was holding up the dish as if to ask for more. His mouth was packed full, and there were molasses-soaked crumbs sticking to his chin.

"Do you want more?"

39

Jacques nodded his head vigorously.

"Say please."

"Blaaaze!"

Several crumbs of ash-cake spewed through Jacques' lips as he spoke. This made him laugh and choke, spewing the whole mouthful. He immediately started crying and shoved the crumbs back into his mouth. He swatted Claire.

"Don't get mad," Claire said laughing, "I'll give you some more."

She cut another piece of ash-cake and drenched it with molasses. Mama would be angry if she saw how much molasses she poured on, but Papa would only laugh.

Jacques dove at the ash-cake and molasses. There was a crazy, wild-animal look in his eyes as he shoved bites of the dripping ash-cake in his mouth.

"Don't eat too fast, Jacques. You might poke your eye out with your spoon."

Jacques laughed again, but this time held his lips tightly together.

"Well Jacques, I'm going to sew. I'll be out front if you need me."

Jacques didn't respond.

Claire picked up the sewing basket and went out the front door. Mosquitos weren't much of a problem this far from the river, so she sat under a huge shady elm and took the shirt for Brother Smith out of the basket.

Papa needs a new shirt, too, she thought after a few moments of stitching. *He only has two. One of them is falling apart, and the other is so thread-bare I can almost see through it.*

I'd rather be sewing a shirt for Papa, she thought, *but Brother Smith will pay thirty cents, and that will buy a lot of meat for Mama.*

Chapter Three

TOWARDS evening Claire sewed the last stitch and tied the last knot in the shirt

"There," she said with obvious satisfaction. She held the shirt up to get a better look at her handiwork. "He might like this so much, he'll pay thirty-five cents."

"Hello!" a voice called out.

It was Papa's voice. Claire looked east toward the river. He wasn't in sight, yet. She dropped the shirt in the basket and started running down the path toward the sound. Immediately, she slowed to a walk.

"Papa," she shouted. "Is that you?"

"Aye, lass."

Brother Nicol emerged from a small thicket. His hands were covered with black smudges of ink. He carried several sheets of scrap newsprint under his arm. Claire continued walking toward him at a slow gait.

"How was your day at *The Wasp*, Papa?"

"We were very busy. We didn't even stop for lunch."

"Well, come in the house, and I'll fix dinner. There's ash-cake already fixed, and I can boil those beet greens you picked yesterday."

"That sounds tasty, but I can't stop working, yet. I have to thin the rest of the beets in the garden. The potatoes are coming up fine. I think we'll have plenty this winter. Maybe I can dig a few up, and you can boil them with the greens for dinner. Where's Jacques and your mother?"

"They're both sleeping in Mama's bed. I told Jacques to go take a nap about an hour ago, and he isn't up yet."

They came near the big elm, and Claire started to run over to get the sewing basket. Immediately, she slowed to a walk.

"I finished that shirt for Brother Smith today," Claire called over her shoulder, picking up the basket. She walked back to her father's side.

"That is good! Now we can buy some meat for your mother."

"And molasses for Jacques," Claire added.

"Aye." Brother Nicol took the shirt out of the basket and held it up. "That's beautiful, lass! You sew almost as well as your mother."

They walked a few more steps in silence.

"I'm going to go work in the garden now. You go start a fire for cooking."

Brother Nicol went to the garden, and Claire continued on to the cabin. She opened

45

the front door and went in. Jacques came out of the bedroom rubbing his eyes.

"Is Papa home?" he asked.

"He came home just now. He's out in the garden."

Jacques walked to the front door still wiping his eyes.

Only an inch or two of ashes were in the fireplace, so Claire just pushed them to one side. She wadded up a sheet of paper Papa brought home from *The Wasp*, place it on the stone floor of the fireplace. She piled on kindling, then lit it. As soon as the flames had grown she piled on sticks, then two small logs. The beet greens had already been washed and fit nicely in the cool water in the spider.

Jacques came back in the cabin. In his hands he held seven very small potatoes.

"Papa said to give you these."

"Have they been washed?"

"I don't know. Papa just gave them to me and told me to give them to you."

He handed the potatoes to Claire. They weren't much larger than large marbles. Small clots of moist soil dotted the skin of each one.

"Can you go to the stream out back and wash them for me?" Claire asked.

"Mama and Papa won't let me go near the stream unless they're with me," Jacques said. "They're afraid I'll fall in."

"Well, come on then."

Claire stood and took Jacques' hand. They left through the back door. In a few moments they returned, closing the door behind themselves. Jacques was laughing and carrying three of the potatoes. Claire was carrying four.

She got a sharp knife off of the clapboard, then began to carve the potatoes into chucks, dropping the pieces into the spider.

"Do you know what this is called, Jacques?" Claire tapped her knife on the rim of the spider.

"That's Hemish the spider!"

"That's right! What a smart boy!"

Jacques smiled proudly.

Claire carefully set the lid on top of the spider, set the pot on top of the fire and piled glowing red coals on top of the lid. She hugged her knees, waiting for jets of steam to shoot out from under the lid.

"Do you want to hear a story, Jacques?" Claire asked.

"No, I heard one already today."

"But this is a special one. It's about a Warlock and a Princess."

"But you told me that one already."

"But this times I'm going to tell it a little different."

"All right. . .," Jacques said slowly.

"All right." Claire paused for a long moment, poking the coals in the fire with a stick.

"Once upon a time," she said in very dramatic and mellow voice. "Once upon a time, there was a beautiful princess named Clara. . .."

"Like you, huh," Jacques said.

"Kind of like me, but her name was Clar-*a* and mine is Claire."

"Oh. . .and she had a twin sister named Marie, right?"

"No, Clara had a twin sister named Mari-*a*. They were kind and good to everyone they met, and all the people of the kingdom loved them like the moon and the stars. People came from miles around just to gaze on the two Princesses.

"And there was a cruel Warlock named Greezerbud. Now Geezerbud hated the princesses, because people loved them and

didn't love him. So one day when the princesses were playing in the garden, Geezerbud put a curse on them. He said, 'As long as the sun shines, you girls shall be weak and feeble of heart.

"That curse made Princess Clara so sick she had to stay in bed for a year and a day. Princess Maria got so sick she died. From then on the King and Queen carried Clara on a pillow all day long, because they were afraid she would get sick again and die like Maria.

"But every night, when the castle was sleeping and the sun wasn't shining, Clara would sneak out into the garden and run. She ran like the wind all night long. When the sky turned into morning, Clara would sneak back into the castle.

"Well, one day Geezerbud decided to try to make the people of the kingdom like him, so he made a big festival with clowns and dancing and parades. And he had a big footrace. He

51

said all the children of the Kingdom could run, and he would grant one wish to the girl or boy who won.

"But Geezerbud really didn't want to grant a wish, so he made the footrace so long no one could ever finish. It would take all day and all night of running for a person to finish--and no one can do that.

"Well, Princess Clara entered the footrace and all day long, while the sun was shining, she could only plod along. But when the night came, she ran faster than the wind--faster than any creature, human or animal, in the whole Kingdom. All night long she passed boys who were sweating and cursing, and girls who were flopping over and crying. In the morning, when she came to the finish line, she was the only person still running.

"Geezerbud got so mad when he saw Clara win that he stomped up and down till his heart exploded from the fury. As soon as Geezerbud died, the curse died with him. Princess Clara became strong again, and her heart became like the heart of a lion. So everyone loved her again, and she lived happily ever after."

"That's a silly story!" Jacques said.

Presently tiny jets of steam shot out from the lid of the spider. Claire eased the lid off and poked a potato with the knife. It was soft.

"I guess dinner's ready," Claire said. "You go get Papa, and I'll take the food into Mama's room. We'll eat in there tonight."

Jacques jumped to his feet and ran out the front door.

Chapter Four

IT was dark outside when Jacques finally fell asleep. He was on his stomach sleeping on his bedroll in front of the hearth. By the light of the glowing embers in the fireplace Claire could see a string of drool falling from Jacques' open mouth. Mama was in her room sleeping. Claire's bedroll was beside Jacques', but she wasn't on it.

Claire was in her night clothes, and she and Brother Nicol were both sitting at the table reading by the flickering light of an oil lamp. Brother Nicol was re-reading the latest copy of *The Time and Seasons*. The Prophet Joseph

Smith had published an important discourse in it which Papa said was fascinating. Claire had read it when her father first brought the paper home, but didn't understand it very well. She was reading a primer about Canadian history.

A knock sounded on the door.

Brother Nicol stood very slowly, eyes still fixed to the paper, and walked hesitantly toward the door. When he stepped out of the light from the lamp, he dropped the paper to his side.

"Coming," he said in a whispering tone.

Claire looked up from her primer and turned her attention toward the door.

"Hello, Brother Jones," Brother Nicol said when he opened the door. "Come in, come in."

Brother Jones was the husband of the only midwife in Zarahemla. He was a huge, furry man. Claire thought he looked like a bear.

"I can't stay," Brother Jones said as soon as he was inside. "I'm taking Sister Jones over to the Prophet's house in Nauvoo. She just came down with ague. She's on a horse out in the front yard. My wife wanted me to tell you that you better find another midwife in Nauvoo to attend the birth. She has a feeling your baby will come early, probably before she has recuperated."

Claire got up from the table and walked toward the front door.

"Aye," Brother Nicol said, "that is wise. But why are you taking her to the Prophet's house? Wouldn't she rest better in her own home?"

"Well, I told Sister Jones the Prophet is a busy man, but she insisted. Once she's made her mind up, Sister Jones is more terrible than an army with banners."

"Aye," Brother Nicol said chuckling, "sounds like Sister Nicol."

They both laughed for a brief moment.

"Anyway," Brother Jones continued, "my wife says a lot of people who have ague go to the Prophet's house to recuperate, and Sister Emma takes care of them. Not many of them die, and those who recover seem to get better faster."

"Papa, do you know any midwives in Nauvoo," Claire asked.

"No, but I'm sure I'll be able to find one."

"Hello, Claire," Brother Jones said. "How are you?"

"I'm fine, thank you. And how are you Brother Bear--I mean, Jones" Claire smiled politely, hiding her embarrassment.

"I'm doing all right." Brother Jones smiled broadly. "I saw you this morning. You were running along side of a great big black mare. You sure run fast--that horse couldn't even keep up with you."

Claire's heart froze within her chest.

57

Now Papa will get mad and punish me for running, she thought.

"Ho, ho, ho," Brother Nicol laughed. "You must be mistaken. Claire had scarlet fever when she was a wee lass, and now she has a feeble heart. She can't run fast like that."

Brother Nicol laughed again.

"Well. . .these poor old eyes of mine have played tricks on me many times," Brother Jones said smiling. "It's not the first time I've been mistaken." He winked at Claire.

Claire smiled politely.

He knows it was me, she thought. *I just hope he can keep a secret. . .at least until the day after tomorrow.*

"I would like to stay longer, but I'm afraid Sister Jones won't stay on that horse much longer before she comes in here with her tongue on fire," Brother Jones said. "Good night to both of you."

"Good night."

"Good night."

Brother Nicol closed the door behind Brother Jones and returned to the table to finish reading. Claire lay down on her bedroll.

"Good night, Papa," she said.

"Good night, lass."

Presently, the oil lamp went out, and Papa went to the bedroom.

Chapter Five

EARLY the next morning Claire went with her father to the cove where the canoe was tied. As usual she rode Jezebel and Papa walked. Papa carried the shirt for Brother William Smith under his arm.

"Lassie," Brother Nicol said, "I want to thank you for sewing this shirt. The midwife said it's very important that your mother get some meat. If she has complications, we might lose her like we lost Marie."

Claire remained silent, not knowing how to respond. Brother Nicol reached up on top of the horse and hugged her around the waist.

"I'll get some meat for dinner, so don't fix anything for tonight."

Brother Nicol led the horse through the grove of trees to the shallow cove where the canoe was tied. Claire swatted furiously, and Jezebel's skin shimmied.

"I know you were counting on going over to Nauvoo for the Fourth of July Celebration," Brother Nicol said. His speech was very hesitant. "But since Sister Jones is sick, I think it would be better if you were to stay home with your mother."

"But, Papa. . .."

"I'm sorry, lass. I would stay myself, but Brother Smith wants all the men who work at *The Wasp* to march in the parade together."

Brother Nicol got into the canoe and started rowing.

"But, Papa," Claire said loudly, "going to the festival is the most important thing in my life."

"I'm sorry, lass."

The current started to carry the boat downstream.

"But, Papa. . .."

The canoe drifted out of sight.

"Could you repeat that, lass? I can't hear you."

"Never mind," Claire yelled.

She pulled on Jezebel's reins until she turned around. The horse started to trot, but Claire reined her back.

"I'm not going to run today," she said. "All that running has been for nothing."

Finally, she tugged the horse to a stop, got off and walked slowly at it's side. She didn't look up from the ground to see the Temple across the river.

Chapter Six

CLAIRE sat in the saddle on Jezebel's back and watched as excited children and their parents crammed onto the two skiffs that had come over from Nauvoo to carry the people from Zarahemla across the wide lazy river. It seemed like everyone in town was on those skiffs, Brother Jones, Sister Knight and her husband, Bishop Jensen and his wife-- everyone except Claire.

The first skiff pushed off the shore.

Jacques and Papa were on the second skiff. Papa was standing near the rear, and Jacques was on his shoulders. Jacques had a smile of wild excitement. Papa seemed excited, too.

"What a glorious day," Papa had said earlier when he, Jacques and Claire left the cabin and walked toward the river. He held Jezebel's reins. Jacques and Claire were riding on her back. Jacques hugged Claire's waist tightly.

"Something is telling me that today is going to be a very special day," Papa said. "Something unbelievable will happen that we will write about in our diaries."

Jacques started to slip, and Brother Nicol paused while he boosted the boy.

"I only wish you could be there when it happens, Claire," he continued with some sadness in his voice.

Something special would happen, if you'd let me go with you, she thought.

The second skiff finally pulled away from the shore. Seven strong men were kneeling on each side paddling. Both Jacques and Papa waved to Claire. She waved back.

"Come on, Jezebel," Claire said when the skiffs were several hundred yards from shore. She twitched the reins, and the old horse started trotting. Claire reined back slightly, slowing the horse to a walk.

"I didn't want to go to that stupid old celebration, anyway," Claire said when she was half way home. "I was born in Canada, so July Fourth is just another day to me--and a stupid one at that. That celebration is for people who were born in the United States."

The old horse snorted as if in agreement. Claire dismounted and walked at the side of the horse.

"I wouldn't feel so bad if I hadn't have spent so much time running to get ready for the races," she muttered.

A faint moan seemed to haunt the trail ahead. The moan sounded like the angry growl of a sow bear. Jezebel pricked her ears forward. Her muscles tensed.

"Did you hear that, Jezebel? That's the sound Mama made when Jacques was born! We better hurry home!"

Claire jumped into the saddle and kicked her heels into Jezebel's flanks as hard as she could. Jezebel seemed to sense danger and lurched into a gallop. Claire had never experienced Jezebel's power before and was tossed backwards in the saddle. She dropped the reins and grabbed the horn with both hands to keep from falling. She wanted to laugh with delight, but anxiety about her mother prevented her. Jezebel galloped like a whirlwind directly toward the cabin.

The horrible moans became silent and didn't start again until Claire was almost at the old elm in the front yard. The sound was more terrible than it was at Jacques' birth. She swung out of the saddle and ran into the cabin.

"Mama, are you all right?" she said before she ran into the bedroom.

"Oh, my sweet baby, Claire," Mama said. Her voice was very distressed. "The baby is coming, and I'm afraid I will die--there's no one here to help me. This pain is much worse than it was in any other birth."

"Don't worry, Mama. I'll go get Papa, and he'll bring a midwife over from Nauvoo. You'll be all right."

The pain seemed to seize Sister Nicol again. Profuse perspiration suddenly covered Mama's face. She moaned again. At first the sound was fearsome, but it quickly became much stronger. Claire felt a great shiver run through her. Perspiration coated her own skin. Shortly, Mama became silent and rested back heavily on her pillow.

A few moments of silence passed before either could speak.

"My poor sweet Claire," Mama finally said, "already you have lost a sister, and now I'm afraid you will lose your mother, too. I am dying."

"Mama, don't be so afraid!" Claire said sharply. "I won't lose you, and I didn't lose Marie, either. When the temple is finished, it won't matter if I'm on this side and Marie's on that side. We'll still be twins, and we'll still be your daughters. If you go to the other side, we'll still be a family--no matter what. So don't be afraid!"

Sister Nicol smiled weakly, then closed her eyes.

"I'm going to get Papa!" Claire bolted out of the room.

Jezebel was standing near the front door, pawing the ground as if she was ready and eager to run like a flash of lightning. Without bothering with the stirrups, Claire leaped up onto her back. She hunkered down over the saddle and dug her heels into the horse's flanks. Jezebel lurched into a gallop.

Claire sat up straight as the horse bolted like a whirlwind toward the river. Before she knew it, they came to the trail where Papa always cut off to get to the canoe. Jezebel turned up the path without Claire even twitching the reins. Half way to the cove she began to falter. Her pace slowed and the sweat on her neck was beginning to lather.

"What's wrong Jezebel?" Claire asked. "Are you getting tired?"

Claire reined the horse to a stop and dismounted. She walked in front of her at a quick pace, pulling the reins behind her. Grampa Molineaux, Mama's father, raised horses and cattle in Canada and taught her to always walk a lathering horse.

"Come on, Jezebel," she said. "We don't want your heart to give in, like Grampa

Molineaux said. We want to cool you off a little before you drink out of the river."

The horse snorted in agreement.

They quickly came to the cove where Papa always tied up the canoe. After tying the reins to a branch that was close to the water, Claire untied the canoe and got in. As she had seen Papa do a hundred times, she knelt in the back and rested her bottom on the narrow slat which crossed the bow. She started paddling with all her strength. The canoe hardly seemed to move.

"I wish I could walk on water," she muttered to herself and dug deeper with the paddle. "Maybe I could cross faster then."

After twenty minutes Claire became very weary. Her arms, shoulders and back burned worse than the coals she piled on Hemish the Spider. Her legs were beginning to cramp, and her knees hurt almost as bad as if she had been kneeling on ice. She began to wonder how far downstream she would drift if she were to stop paddling. She wondered if she would be carried all the way down to the Gulf of Mexico.

"No," Claire mumbled, "I'll just rest for a minute.

Claire set the paddle inside the canoe and, resting her full weight on the slat beneath her bottom, straightened out her knees. She stretched her arms above her head even though they felt like lead. It felt good. She folded her arms on her knees and rested her head.

With her eyes closed she began to think about Grampa Molineaux. Before Claire and Marie got the fever, sometimes Papa and Mama would let them spend the whole day out on Grampa Molineaux's ranch. Spending the day was always best at a calving time. The calves were so fun to watch. They were so happy and playful, running, jumping and dancing. Sometimes Grampa Molineaux

71

would take Claire and Marie into the barn and let them help feed the orphan calves whose mothers had died giving birth. It was so happy to feed the calves. Their warm tongues licking Claire's hands, and their skinny bodies rubbing against her hips.

Claire was always excited to go feed the orphan calves, but Marie didn't like it. She said the orphan calves always had a frighten look in their eyes, and they were smaller and weaker than the other calves.

"These calves don't do very well without their mothers," Grampa Molineaux said one time. "Nothing does well without a mother."

Claire jolted upright.

"Nothing does well without a mother," Grampa Molineaux's voice seemed to say. The words pierced her to the heart.

Startled, Claire looked over her shoulders. The voice was so clear and penetrating it sounded like Grampa Molineaux was sitting in the canoe with Claire.

Claire picked up the paddle and dug it into the water with new strength and determination.

"Jacques needs a mother," Claire muttered to herself. "So do I, and so does the new baby. If Mama goes to the other side, we'll still be a family in the next world. But, Jacques can't wait till then. He needs a mother right now."

Chapter Seven

CLAIRE had to drift downstream for almost two hundred yards along the Illinois bank before she found a cove where she could land the canoe. She tied the boat securely to the trunk of a small tree and waded to shore. She walked up to a dusty road near the cove and looked in either direction, trying to find Nauvoo.

I probably drifted farther than Papa would have, because he rows faster and I'm lighter, Claire thought, thinking like a Scotsman. *So Nauvoo is probably up the river a ways.*

She reached down between her ankle for the back hem of her skirt and pulled it up to her waist, making britches. She started to run, but her knees had grown stiff and achy from kneeling in the canoe. She slowed to a fast walk.

There was a small hill in the road, and from the crest Claire could see the unfinished Temple on the hill above Nauvoo. She could hear the faint sounds of brass bands playing and of guns popping in the air. She saw small clouds of gun smoke drifting after each volley of gunfire.

"Nothing does well without a mother," she felt Grampa Molineaux say to her heart. "Nothing does well without a mother."

Claire tried to run again. This time her knees didn't ache or feel stiff. It felt easy to run as if she were rolling down a hill. She felt free like a bird again. The wind pressed lightly against her cheeks. Her legs felt strong, and she pressed on a little faster.

A flatbed wagon, used for hauling lumber, appeared on the road ahead. Many children and few women were sitting on the wagon, and a few men walked at the side of it. One of the boys pointed as Claire ran passed and yelled, "Look at that girl running! Her legs are showing!"

Claire had no time to be embarrassed. She simply dropped the handful of skirt in her hand and continued running, leaving the wagon behind.

A few houses came into view. When she came to them she turned toward the Temple. A crowd of boys about her own age were standing in the road listening to a man speaking. He lifted his arm into the air and brought it down. All of the boys started running toward the Temple. Claire quickly

caught up with the boys and ran passed eight of them.

"Hey, you can't run!" the one of them yelled. "You're a girl!"

Claire didn't have time to stop and argue. She sped passed five more boys. Only ten more were still in her way.

The Temple was getting closer, and Claire could see a host of people standing where the road started to climb the hill to the unfinished building. The people were cheering and had strung a wide paper ribbon across the road. Claire ran passed four more boys.

Where am I going to find Papa? she thought. She passed two more boys. *I didn't know there would be so many people here.* She passed three more boys.

"Papa!" Claire yelled into the crowd. "Papa!"

"Claire!" Papa's voice said.

The sound came from the other side of the paper ribbon. There was still one boy ahead of Claire and he broke through the ribbon. He dropped to his hands and knees, then rolled onto his back, panting heavily.

"Papa!" Claire yelled.

"Claire, what are you doing?" Papa came out of the crowd carrying Jacques on his shoulders. He had an angry expression.

The other boys ran through the ribbon, and most of them fell down panting.

"How many times have I told you not to run? You could get sick again. And why did you leave your mother at home alone? That was a very selfish thing to do."

"I'm sorry, Papa," Claire said between breaths. "But the baby is coming, and Mama needs help. I just came to find you."

"All the way from Zarahemla--alone?"

"Yes, Papa, but let's find a midwife."

"I'm a midwife," a fat woman with red skin said from the crowd of people. "My name is Sister O'Brien, and this is my husband, Brother O'Brien. He's a ferryman. He can get us across the river to Zarahemla, if that's where your mother is."

"Thank you," Claire and Brother Nicol said almost in unison.

"You can borrow my wagon to get to the ferry," a man in the crowd said. "I'm Brother Green, and I've got the fastest team in Nauvoo. They're probably not as fast as your little girl, but they'll do."

"Thank you," Brother Nicol said. "Where is your team now?"

"Right over there." The man pointed to a field where two horses were grazing. "I'll go get them." Brother Green started running. Brother Nicol took Jacques off his shoulders.

"You stay here with Claire," he said. "I'm going to help with the horses." He ran toward the field.

"I'll go get a crew together," Brother O'Brien, the ferryman, said.

"And get my baby satchel from home!" the midwife yelled after him.

"Is Mama sick?" Jacques asked.

"She's going to have a baby," Claire answered. "We've got to get back home so we can help her."

"Oh." Jacques seemed to be satisfied with that answer.

"How far is your mother along?" Sister O'Brien asked.

"A little more than seven and a half months, I think," Claire said. "Sister Jones, the midwife before, was worried that Mama might have complications and told her to eat some fresh meat every day. We couldn't get any till

81

last night, so I don't know if it will do any good."

"Don't worry, Girl," the midwife said. "The Prophet Joseph Smith, himself, set me apart to be a midwife, and in the blessing he said I would call on the powers of Heaven to remedy any situation, if it be the Lord's will. Don't worry about a thing."

The ferryman came running, carrying a small black leather bag. Five stout young men were running behind him. They all looked as big as Brother Jones.

"I got a crew," he said. "Let's go to the ferry."

"Wait," the midwife said. "They went to hitch up a wagon and a fast team."

"It will take us longer to cross if we take a team and a wagon on board."

"But how will I get to their house fast, if we don't take a good team with us?" the midwife asked.

"I have an old mare tied up on the other bank," Claire said. "You and I could ride her."

"Is she fast?"

"Well, she's blind in one eye, but she can run like a whirlwind."

"That's good enough."

Papa and the man with the wagon suddenly appeared as if from no where. A pair of young black geldings pulled the wagon. There was fire in their eyes, and their shoulders and chests were heavy with muscle.

"Get in!" Papa yelled.

The ferryman and his crew and the midwife piled in. Claire lifted Jacques onto Papa's lap, next to the driver, then got in herself. With a flick of the reins the horses bolted toward the river. When they came to the dusty road along the bank, the ferryman signaled to Brother Green, saying the ferry landing was upstream. Brother Green turned the horses north.

"Is this all the faster these horses can go?" Jacques asked Brother Green, the driver. "My sister can run faster than this!"

Brother Green grinned as if Jacques had told him a joke.

"Aye, that she can, laddie," Papa said. "But these horses have got to pull a heavy wagon with eleven people in it,"

"Oh."

Brother Green reined the horses to a stop, and everyone piled out and ran to the ferryboat.

"Thank you," Claire said as she climbed out of the wagon.

"Aye, thank you," Brother Nicol yelled. He carried Jacques under one arm like a cord of wood.

"Glad to help," Brother Green said. "Will you need the horses on the other side?"

"We have a horse waiting there," Claire yelled back, " but thanks again."

Brother Green smiled and waved. He turned the horse to go back to Nauvoo.

The ferryman and his crew took their positions on either side of the boat, and waited for the others to board. Sister O'Brien, the portly midwife, was the last to waddle aboard.

Brother O'Brien gave a command, and the crew dipped their oars in to water. He began chanting a song, and the crew chanted back and rowed rhythmically. The ferryboat gained speed until it seemed to hum across the water. Claire was very surprised at how fast the boat moved.

Brother Nicol sat on a wooden bench at the side of Sister O'Brien. Jacques sat on one knee, and Claire sat on the other.

"That was a fearsome thing you did, lass, crossing the Mississippi by yourself," Brother Nicol said. "You have the heart of a lion, you do."

Chapter Eight

THE ferryboat landed about two hundred yards from the cove where Jezebel was tied. As soon as the ferry touched the shore, Brother Nicol jumped off with a rope in his hand and tied it around the trunk of a large tree. Brother O'Brien threw him a second rope. The crew all slumped over their oars, breathing heavily. They all looked like they were about to start lathering.

Claire jumped off of the ferry and ran to get Jezebel. The horse stood under a tree placidly munching the grass. The lather on her neck had dried and become crusty.

"Jezebel, is that you?" Claire asked.

The horse looked up and snorted. There was fire in her good eye, and to Claire she appeared as muscular as Brother Green's geldings.

"Jezebel, you have the heart of a lion, don't you?" she said with delight.

The horse tossed her head and stomped her foot on the ground.

Claire ran to the horse, untied the reins and jumped in the saddle. She rode back to the spot where the ferry had landed. Papa and Sister O'Brien were impatiently waiting under a tree. Papa was holding Jacques under one arm.

Claire stopped the horse and jumped off.

"Do you think that poor old horse can carry me?" Sister O'Brien asked.

"She's got a whirlwind inside of her," Claire said. "I bet she could pull a wagon even faster than those two geldings in Nauvoo."

87

Papa helped Sister O'Brien into the saddle, then set Claire in back of her.

"Don't sweat the horse, lass. I'm afraid Sister O'Brien might fall off." Papa gave Jezebel a gentle swat on the flank.

The horse began trotting.

"I can run faster than this," Claire said after a few hundred yards.

"Well, hold on tight girl," Sister O'Brien said. "I've been riding since I was three-years-old. We're going to see that whirlwind you've been talking about." She whipped the end of the reins against Jezebel's flanks and continued whipping.

Jezebel seemed startled for a second, then lurched into a gallop full bore. She turned up the road to the cabin.

"We're going to have to get off about a hundred yards from the cabin and walk Jezebel," Claire yelled. "I think she'll overheat."

"Maybe we can ride right up to the cabin," Sister O'Brien yelled back. "I can go in to your mother, and you can walk the horse for a minute."

"All right."

Jezebel turned off the main road and galloped up the trail to the cabin. They heard Mama moaning, but this time the sound was more like an intensely pained wail.

"I hope we get there in time," Sister O'Brien yelled, "sounds like the baby is about to come." She whipped Jezebel again.

The horse ran at an even faster speed, and they were quickly at the cabin. Sister O'Brien gracefully swung off of the horse and ran in. Claire jumped off and took the reins in one hand. She began to walk the horse back down the trail. Jezebel seemed reluctant to move, so Claire tugged especially hard. The horse began to walk, stepping heavily.

After they had walked for a few moments, Claire led the horse to the stream out back. Jezebel dropped her head and took a long, slow drink. Claire dropped onto her hands and knees and took a drink herself, sticking her face in the water upstream from the horse.

Suddenly, a baby's cry filled the air.

Jezebel lifted her head and pricked her ears.

"Do you hear that, Jezebel?" Claire asked in an excited voice. "That's our new little sister or maybe another brother."

"Girl!" Sister O'Brien's voice rang out. "Come here! I need you!"

Claire jumped to her feet and ran into the cabin.

"What do you want me to do?" she asked as she walked into the bedroom.

"I want you to dry off the baby and make sure it keeps breathing. I'm going to be busy with your mother. She's got complications."

Claire froze at the dreadful word.

Mama was covered with sweat. Her eyes were closed, and she seemed very groggy as if she were drunken.

"Is she all right?"

"She will be, if I can stop the complications. Now dry off the baby and keep it warm. If the baby gets cold it may get sick-- use your petticoats." Sister O'Brien opened her black baby satchel and got a bundle of scorched cloths.

Claire reached down for the hem of her skirt and pulled out her petticoats. She took the handsome baby from the midwife's arm and began drying.

"Is it a boy or a girl?" she asked.

"I don't know. I didn't have time to check."

Claire quickly checked as she was drying. It was a boy. She dried off the back of the baby's head, then wrapped him in a clean blanket at the foot of the bed and held him close. He had red hair like Papa. The baby soon closed his eyes and stopped crying. He nuzzled close to Claire's chest.

Claire sat on the side of the bed and stared at Sister O'Brien. She was holding one hand up toward the ceiling and had the other hand on Mama's belly. Her lips were moving, but Claire couldn't hear any words. She dropped a hand to her waist and and quickly pulled the other away from Mama's belly.

"There," Sister O'Brien said, "your mother will be fine. Thanks be to the Lord."

"Thanks be to the Lord," Claire repeated. "It's a boy," she said in an excited voice and held the baby up for the midwife to see.

Sister O'Brien took the baby and hugged him warmly. She set him gently on Mama's chest with his face toward her neck. Mama opened her eyes briefly, smiled faintly, then closed them again.

"He's a beautiful boy, Sister Nicol," the midwife said. "And thanks to your daughter, you're both alive."

Mama smiled weakly with her eyes shut.

"I don't know why," Claire said slowly with a yawn, "but suddenly I'm awfully tired."

"Of course, you are," Sister O'Brien said. "Anyone would be tired after rowing across the river and running all that way to Nauvoo. Why don't you lie down next to your mother and rest a bit?"

Claire put her head on the pillow next to her mother's and stared at the baby. He had such a beautiful, soft and wise glow to his face.

"That's a beautiful baby, Mama," Claire said quietly.

Mama smiled weakly.

Claire closed her eyes, but before she could fall asleep, Papa came into the room. He was carrying Jacques on his back.

"How's my wife?" he asked the midwife.

"She's fine, but we would have lost her if your daughter wasn't as brave and strong as she is."

"Aye," Papa said, "Claire's a fine lass."

"Is it a brother or a sister," Jacques asked.

"It's a boy."

"Then we're going to name him Hemish, right Papa?"

"No, laddie," Papa said. "Hemish is a silly name. We're going to name him Clairence."